S0-ALI-415

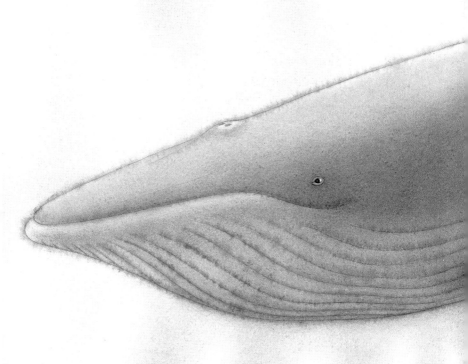

For Davy Sidjanski

First mini-book edition published in the United States, Great Britain,
Canada, Australia, and New Zealand in 2002 by North-South Books,
an imprint of Nord-Süd Verlag AG, Gossau Zürich, Switzerland.
Distributed in the United States by North-South Books Inc., New York

ISBN 0-7358-1953-X
1 3 5 7 9 10 8 6 4 2
Printed in China

RAINBOW FISH
AND THE **BIG BLUE WHALE**

MARCUS PFISTER

TRANSLATED BY J. ALISON JAMES

NORTH-SOUTH BOOKS
NEW YORK/LONDON

A long way out in the deep
blue sea, Rainbow Fish and his
friends swam happily through
the reef. Each of them had a
glittering silver scale—except
for one little striped fish, but he
belonged to the group anyway.

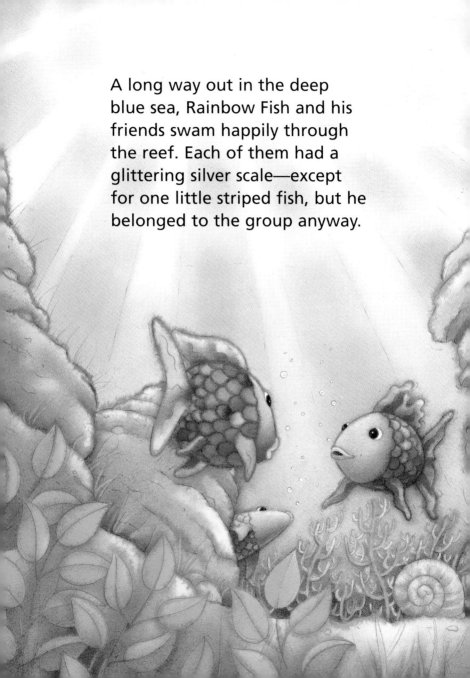

When the fish were hungry, they ate tiny krill. There seemed to be endless supplies of the delicious shrimp. Rainbow Fish only needed to glide gently through the water with his mouth open to catch as many as he wanted. It was a wonderful life.

One day a gentle old whale swam by the reef and decided to stay. He liked the spot, since he too ate the krill that were so plentiful there. And he enjoyed being around the glittering fish. Often he drifted along, watching them for hours, admiring their beautiful silvery scales.

Before long, the fish with the jagged fins noticed the whale watching them.

"Why is he looking at us like that?" he asked the others. He was in a particularly bad mood that day. "See how he's staring at us?" he went on irritably. "Who knows what he's thinking?"

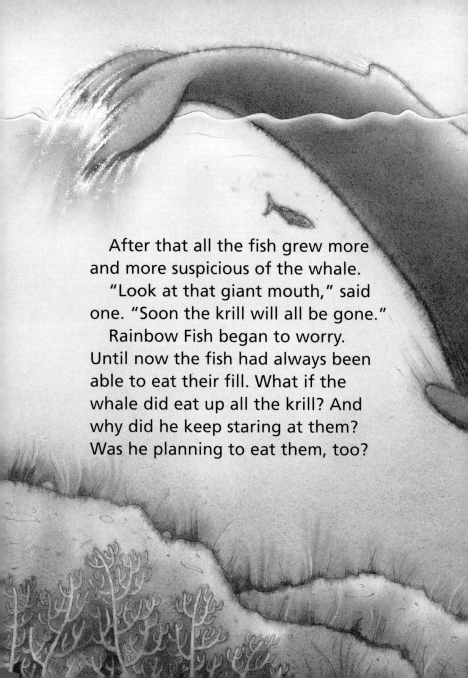

After that all the fish grew more and more suspicious of the whale.

"Look at that giant mouth," said one. "Soon the krill will all be gone."

Rainbow Fish began to worry. Until now the fish had always been able to eat their fill. What if the whale did eat up all the krill? And why did he keep staring at them? Was he planning to eat them, too?

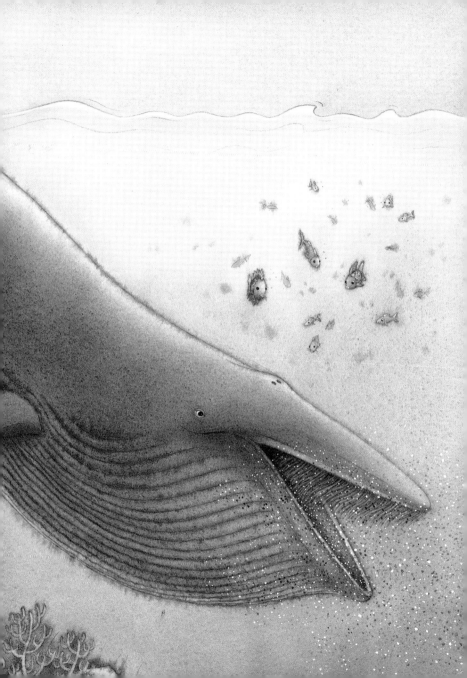

One day the whale swam quite near the school of glittering fish. Panicked, the fish with the jagged fins sounded the alarm.

"Look out!" he called. "The wicked whale is after us!"

When the whale heard that, he was hurt at first, but soon he grew very angry.

I'll show them! he thought. I'll teach them a lesson!

So the great blue whale shot into the middle of the school and lashed out with his gigantic tail, sweeping the sparkling fish in all directions.

The terrified fish fled, racing
towards a crack in the reef for
safety. But the whale didn't
leave them alone. He followed
Rainbow Fish and his friends all
the way back to their cave.

The blue whale swam back and forth, casting sinister glances at the little fish.

They were trapped!

"I told you that whale was dangerous," whispered the fish with the jagged fins. "We have to watch out for him!"

After a while the whale calmed down. He made one last pass, then disappeared behind the reef.

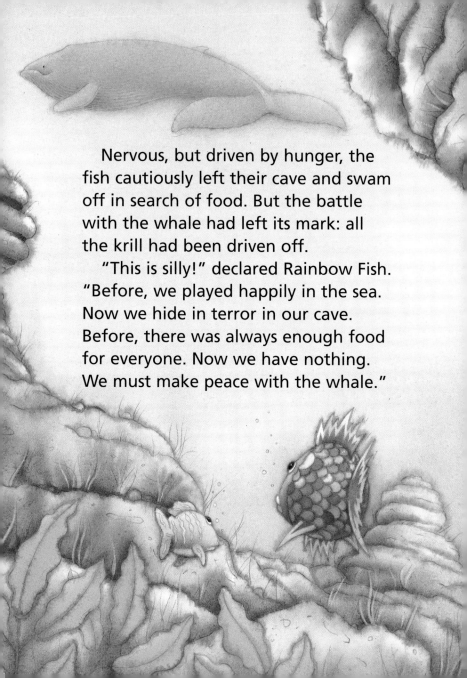

Nervous, but driven by hunger, the fish cautiously left their cave and swam off in search of food. But the battle with the whale had left its mark: all the krill had been driven off.

"This is silly!" declared Rainbow Fish. "Before, we played happily in the sea. Now we hide in terror in our cave. Before, there was always enough food for everyone. Now we have nothing. We must make peace with the whale."

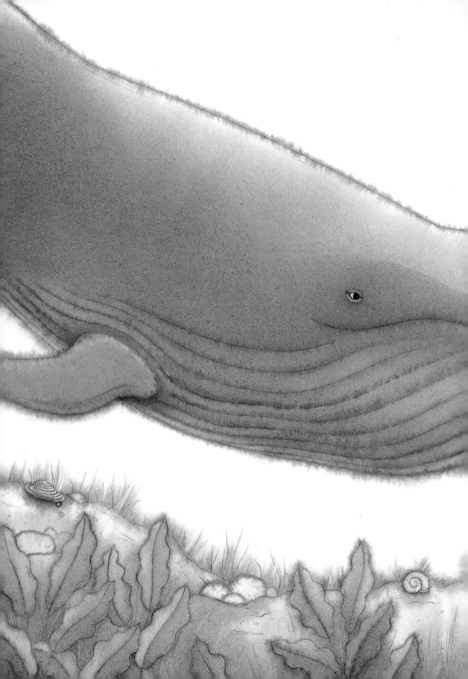

The other fish were all too afraid
to approach the whale. It was up to
Rainbow Fish.

The whale stared at Rainbow Fish
suspiciously.

"Please, let's talk," said Rainbow
Fish. "This fight was all a big
mistake. It drove off the krill and
now we're all hungry."

The two talked for a long time.

The whale told Rainbow Fish how hurt and angry their hostile words had made him. "I never meant to harm you," said the whale, "just scare you a little."

Rainbow Fish was ashamed. "I'm sorry," he said. "But when we saw you watching us all the time, we were afraid you might eat us."

The whale looked surprised. "I watched you only because your shining scales are so pretty," he said.

They both laughed.

"Come now," said the whale. "Let's find new hunting grounds."

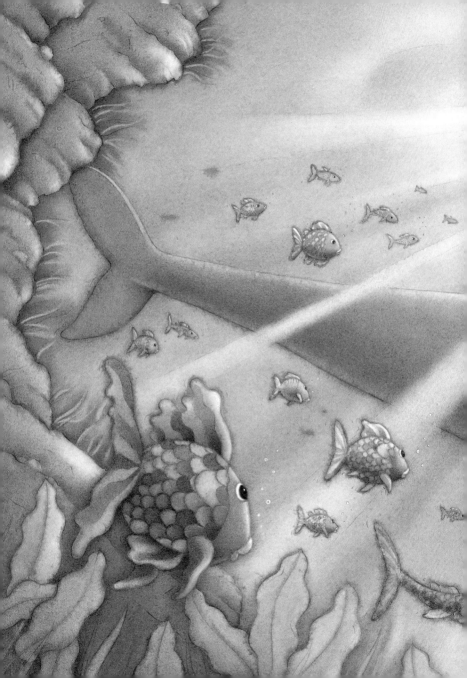

So Rainbow Fish and his friends, protected by their new friend the big blue whale, swam off together in search of a new home rich with krill. And before long, none of them could remember what the terrible fight had been about.

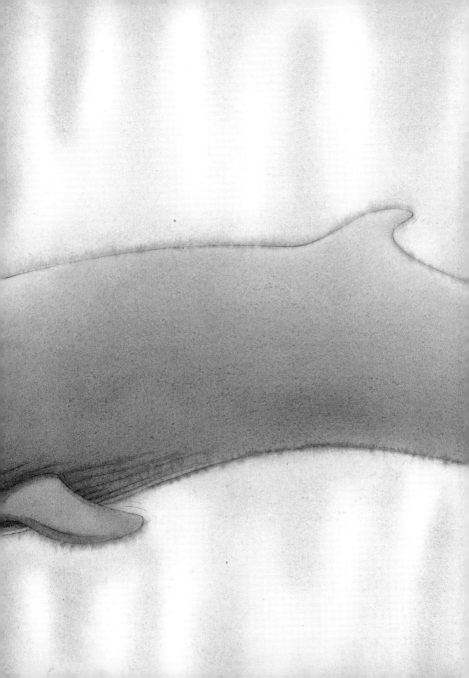